Buzzbee The Magician

GROSSET & DUNLAP
Published by the Penguin Group
Penguin Group (USA) LLC, 375 Hudson Street, New York, New York 10014, USA

USA | Canada | UK | Ireland | Australia | New Zealand | India | South Africa | China

penguin.com
A Penguin Random House Company

ISBN 978-0-448-48694-9

10 9 8 7 6 5 4 3 2 1

"Look what I found, Buzzbee!" said Pappa Bee excitedly.

"It's . . . a hat," Buzzbee said with a shrug.

"It's not just any old hat," said Pappa Bee. "It's my *magic* hat.

Look—there's nothing in it, see?"

Buzzbee nodded. Pappa Bee waved his hand over the hat, then reached inside.

"Ta-da!"

He pulled out a wand and held it in his hand.

"Whoa!" said Buzzbee, his eyes wide. "How did you do that?"

Pappa Bee waved the wand and said in a deep voice, "Abracadabra!"

He reached into the hat again, and this time he pulled out a bunch of flowers.

"It really *is* magic!" cried Buzzbee, buzzing over to Pappa Bee. "Let me try!"

"It takes time to get it right, Buzzbee," Pappa Bee warned him.

"I'm sure I can do it," Buzzbee replied. "I'm going to go practice in my room."

"Ladies, gentlemen, and teddy bees," Buzzbee announced, "here comes some magic!"

He swirled the wand over the hat. "Abracadabra!"

Buzzbee peeked into the hat and frowned. It was empty. He closed his eyes and tried again.

"Abracadabra!"

The hat was *still* empty. This time, Buzzbee tried his best deep magician's voice. "ABRACADABRA!" he boomed.

That didn't work, either. Buzzbee couldn't figure out what he was doing wrong.

Buzzbee went back to Pappa Bee. "I don't think I'm very magic," he said sadly.

Pappa Bee smiled. "You don't have to *be* magic, Buzzbee." He took the hat and pointed inside. "See the bottom there? It's a secret door—you can hide things behind it. When you pull things out of the hat, it looks like you're making them appear out of nowhere!"

"Ooh! Let me try!" Buzzbee exclaimed. He hid Teddy Bee in the hat and waved his wand. "Abracadabra . . . and . . . ta-da!" Teddy Bee magically appeared.

Pappa clapped. "Perfect, Buzzbee!"

"I'm a magician!" cried Buzzbee. "I'm going to put on a magic show for my friends."

That afternoon, Buzzbee performed for Jasper, Barnabee, and Babee.

He showed them the inside of the empty hat. Then he waved his wand and said, "Abracadabra!" in his deep magician's voice.

Abracadabra!

"Ta-da!" he announced, pulling Teddy Bee out of the hat.

Babee bounced around excitedly.

Buzzbee put Teddy Bee back into the hat and waved his wand again.

"Abracadabra!" he said, and Teddy Bee disappeared behind the secret door.

"Wow!" Jasper exclaimed.

"You really *are* magic!" Barnabee marveled.

Suddenly, Rubee's bedroom door opened.

"Oh!" Rubee said. "You've got Pappa's magic hat. Have you shown them the secret door inside?"

She tipped the hat upside down, and Teddy Bee tumbled out.

"Rubee!" Buzzbee yelled.

"So you're not magic after all, Buzzbee," said Barnabee.

Rubee looked at the floor.

"Oops! I'm sorry, Buzzbee. I didn't mean to give away the trick."

"You've spoiled everything, Rubee!" Buzzbee shouted. "I wish *you* would disappear!" And he angrily buzzed off to his room.

Barnabee followed Buzzbee to his room. “Are you okay, Buzzbee?” Barnabee asked.
“No!” Buzzbee replied. “Rubee ruined my show!”
“I don’t think she meant to,” Barnabee said. “Rubee was just being a big sister. Big sisters like to explain *everything*.”

Buzzbee thought about that for a minute. “Maybe you’re right,” he said, sighing. “I’d better go say I’m sorry for shouting.”

Buzzbee and Barnabee went to find Rubee in her room, but she wasn't there.

Then they looked in the living room, but she wasn't there, either.

Finally, Buzzbee went to the playground. "Rubee!" he called, but he couldn't find her anywhere.

"It's like she's disappeared," Buzzbee said to himself. Then he gasped. "Oh no! *I've* made Rubee disappear!"

Buzzbee rushed to his room to get the magic hat.

"I've got to magic her back!" he said. He tried and tried to bring his sister back, but the wand and his special "Abracadabra!" didn't work.

"What if I never see her again?" he moaned. Buzzbee didn't know what to do.

He decided to go to Pappa Bee
to ask for help.

“I’ve done a bad thing, Pappa. I’ve
made Rubee disappear!”

Pappa Bee chuckled. “That’s
impossible, Buzzbee.”

“Then where is she?” Buzzbee cried.

A moment later, Barnabee flew in. “Found her!” he announced as Rubee buzzed into the room behind him.

“Rubee!” Buzzbee said with a big smile. He buzzed happily around his sister. “I’m sorry I shouted at you,” he said. “Where did you go?”

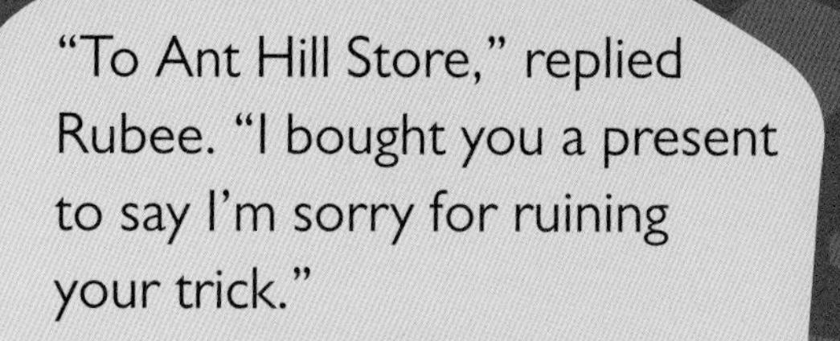

"To Ant Hill Store," replied Rubee. "I bought you a present to say I'm sorry for ruining your trick."

Buzzbee looked at his present. "What is it?"

"It's a new magic trick. You can show it to your friends," Rubee said.

Later that day,
Buzzbee and Rubee
put on a magic show.

"In this magic box, we have our little sister, Babee," Buzzbee announced. He waved his wand around in a circle.

"Abracadabra!" Buzzbee and Rubee said together. Then they opened the box. "TA-DAAA!" Babee was in two pieces!

The audience cheered and clapped.

"Wow!" Jasper exclaimed.

Barnabee looked closely at the little feet poking out of the box. "I've never noticed how much Babee's feet look like a teddy bee's feet . . . ," he said.

"Would our clever magicians and their friends like some honey cake?" Mamma Bee asked.

"Yum!" Buzzbee said excitedly. "For our next trick, we will make it disappear!"